Lee Aucoin, *Creative Director*
Jamey Acosta, *Senior Editor*
Heidi Fiedler, *Editor*
Produced and designed by
Denise Ryan & Associates
Illustration © Karen Eramus
Rachelle Cracchiolo, *Publisher*

Teacher Created Materials

5301 Oceanus Drive
Huntington Beach, CA 92649-1030
http://www.tcmpub.com
ISBN: 978-1-4807-3324-4
© 2014 Teacher Created Materials
Reprinted 2014
Made in China
Nordica.122014. CA21401530

The Untold Story of Ms. Mirabella

Written by Sally Odgers
Illustrated by Karen Erasmus

Ms. Mirabella wore sensible shoes, and her hair was gray around the edges. Her favorite word was *interesting*.

"Words are very interesting," said Ms. Mirabella on Friday. "For instance, consider the word *run*. It's very short, but if you add more letters, you can make other words. When I go *running*, I am a *runner*."

William and Rosalyn laughed. Teachers as old as Ms. Mirabella didn't run. They walked or drove cars.

"Next week, we'll get into pairs and write stories about running," said Ms. Mirabella.

"Cool!" said Rosalyn. She picked up her school bag and turned to William. "We can write about my Uncle Matt. He's going to be in that big race tomorrow."

"Let's go watch," said William. "It will be research for our story."

When Rosalyn went home, she told her dad what William had said.

"I'll take you two to the park to watch the runners go by," said Dad.

Rosalyn hurried next door to tell William the news. "Ms. Mirabella will be so impressed with our research!" she said happily.

"We'll have to think of an interesting title for our story," said William.

On Saturday morning, Rosalyn put on her tennis shoes to walk to the park. "Uncle Matt will be so surprised when he sees us!" she said.

"He might not notice," warned Dad. "He'll be focusing on the race."

The park was crowded with people. Most of them had come to watch the race. The competitors wore shirts with numbers pinned to the front of them.

"I wish I could run in a big race," said Rosalyn, "but I'm not very fast."

Dad laughed. "That doesn't matter a bit, Rosalyn. Lots of people run just for fun. We could all enter a race next month. What do you think?"

Rosalyn hugged herself. "That would be cool, Dad. Let's start training now!"

The park became more crowded. Music poured from the loudspeakers. Rosalyn and William were glad they had come early, because they had a good view of the track. They watched people with numbers going down to one end of the park.

"The starting line is down at the first gate," Dad said. "They go all the way around the park twice and then finish back at the start. Watch carefully, and we might see Uncle Matt go past twice."

The music stopped and the loudspeakers crackled. "Ready!" boomed a voice. "On your marks…get set…go!"

A cheer rang out as the race began.

15

Rosalyn couldn't see the runners yet, but she felt the excitement in the air. *I'll remember this for our story,* she thought.

William jumped up and down. "Here they come!" he yelled.

The first runners flashed past. Rosalyn hardly had time to cheer. More followed, and then a large pack ran by. "Uncle Matt! Uncle Matt!" yelled Rosalyn. "Look, Dad, there's Uncle Matt!" Her uncle flashed her a grin as he raced past.

"He's not going fast enough to win," said William.

"But he's having fun," said Rosalyn.

"There goes Sarah!" said Dad as a young woman ran by. "She works with me at the bank."

Rosalyn wished she were in the race, too. She imagined how it would feel to run with all the others. She was watching the next group of runners to see if they were having fun when she gasped and grabbed William's arm.

"William! That was Ms. Mirabella!"

"What?" William pulled away. "No, it can't be."

Rosalyn blinked. "It looked like her," she said.

"No way," said William. "Ms. Mirabella is too old to run in a race."

"I suppose so." Rosalyn leaned against the fence and watched as the last runners came by. She waved to them, and they grinned and waved back.

"Here come the leaders again," said Dad.

Rosalyn leaned forward and looked hard at the runners. She saw Uncle Matt again and Sarah from the bank. She peered so hard her eyes hurt. "Look!" she said to William.

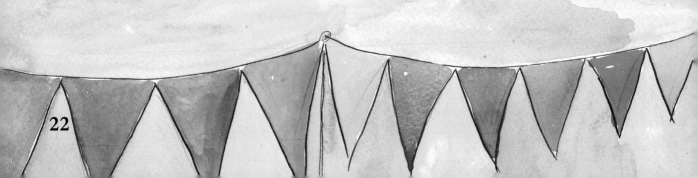

"Look there…the one in the pink shirt. It *is* Ms. Mirabella. It really is!"

William stared. "You're right!"

Rosalyn jumped up and down. "Go, Ms. Mirabella! You can do it!"

"Hurray!" yelled William. "Hurray for Ms. Mirabella!"

Ms. Mirabella must have heard them, for she waved as she ran past.

"That was our teacher!" Rosalyn said to Dad.

"Really? Why didn't you tell me she was in the race?" Dad asked.

"We didn't know!" said Rosalyn. She nudged William and said something else, but cheers from the other end of the park drowned her voice. The winners had crossed the line.

"What did you say?" asked William.

"I have a cool name for our story!" said Rosalyn. "We can call it *The Untold Story of Ms. Mirabella!*"